Vigilis

Biblical, Volume 2

Liam Robert Mullen

Published by Liam Robert Mullen, 2023.

VIGILIS

First edition. November 16, 2023.

ISBN: 979-8223662129

Written by Liam Robert Mullen.

Table of Contents

PROLOGUE.. 1
CHAPTER 1. 4
CHAPTER 2. 10
CHAPTER 3. 20
CHAPTER 4. 25
CHAPTER 5. 28
CHAPTER 6. 32
CHAPTER 7. 35
CHAPTER 8. 40
CHAPTER 9. 44
CHAPTER 10. 47
CHAPTER 11. 51
CHAPTER 12. 54
CHAPTER 13. 58
CHAPTER 14. 62
CHAPTER 15. 66
CHAPTER 16. 69
CHAPTER 17. 76
CHAPTER 18. 87

PROLOGUE

1,800 BC.

Astrology had its roots in the Babylonian culture, far, far back in antiquity. It was a practice indulged in by those who perceived themselves as having a higher calling. Nabu was one such man.

At sixty-three he was no longer a young man and he could feel it in his bones every time he moved. Only the cold grey eyes indicated a sense of mirth, a sense of merriment, a sense of life as he strived to explain drawings to the seven children crowded around him. Like children everywhere they too were full of merriment. Nabu had practised astrology since he was a child no older than those crowded around him.

It was a way of life that had transformed his very existence. His face was wizened by the sun and had seen better days and his fingernails were long on his equally wizened hands. His nose was crooked above a lantern jaw. His dress was that of the land - leather sandals, a white gallibaya, and a silk, sometimes colourful, headscarf, a keffiyeh.

He wiped a bead of sweat from his lined forehead. He had predicted many happy things in his life - his marriage to Gula, whose very name was associated with medicine and the goddess of healing, his three children, two boys and a girl, and a long, happy life.

"What's that, teacher?" one of the brightest boys pointed out.

Nabu smiled. "That's a great question, Nebuchadnezzar."

The ability to discern celestial cycles was a divinatory practice and could be complex. It involved studying the sky and celestial objects and determining future events based on those readings. The practice spread to other countries and cultures and India practiced jyotisha, and China also took it up. The conquests of Alexander the Great allowed the practice to spread into Ancient Greece and later Rome itself, and further areas of Europe.

The boy had pointed at a map which showed the trajectory of the planet Mars over a given time period and how that trajectory might affect future events. There were a number of such maps, diaries which were known as ephemeris containing tables of values. Predictions were then made using mathematical formulae amongst other things.

Nabu explained things slowly, watching for the dawning of light and comprehension in his student's eyes. Comprehension could be slow arriving at times given the complexity of the subject matter.

It had taken Nabu himself years to fully grasp the principles, years of dogged hard work.

Ever since he had been a young boy, he always had an interest in the stars and in future events. He loved Babylon with its ancient riches, hanging gardens and the Temple of Learning. He couldn't have lived anywhere else. He had studied the Hassite dynasty, a time which had heralded great texts in mathematics, medicine and astrology. It was a period of rule over a span of four hundred years. Hammurabi, an Amorite prince, really began the history of Babylon in 1792 BC. Using the threat of war and his diplomatic skills he subdued all of Mesopotamia by 1755 BC and his land was known as Babylonia. In 1595 BC the Hittites sacked his city, and then the Hassites, mountain folk from Persia, conquered the land. Assyrians controlled the land from 911 to 608 BC and after the fall of their empire a Chaldean king took over and began repairing the city from damage caused by the Assyrians, and the work was continued by his son King Nebuchadnezzar 11, who completed work on the hanging gardens, the Tower of Bable, and the Ishtar gate. Nabu looked at the boy who bore the same name as their king and he smiled. The fruit of knowledge could only grow.

He had predicted that Babylon wouldn't last, something the people hadn't wanted to hear.

The pain in his chest was sudden and unexpected.

He gasped for air. He fell.

No longer breathing. Dead.

It was one thing he hadn't predicted.

Death.

Maps and papers lay scattered in the dust.

Nebuchadnezzar bent to gather them, clutching them tightly to his chest. They were his now. Let anyone else try and claim them, then there would be a fight to the finish.

CHAPTER 1.

40^{AD.} The emperor Caligula had succeeded Tiberius three years ago and was only on the throne a short time when the seer came to see him. The seer looked a little unkempt, wild dark hair, hazel eyes that shifted constantly. Neither tall nor short he could have been passed in the Great Forum as a mere nobody. The man had just crossed that great square because everyone knew where the offices of Caligula lay.

For his part, the emperor couldn't have looked more different and one didn't have to look far to see the trappings of power. He was relatively young to hold such high office; late twenties, a pale countenance, tall but with a slender neck and similar legs, somewhat ill -shaped almost like he was ill. His hair was thin and bald at the crown, again signifying he wasn't in the best of health.

He was in an expansive mood having spent the morning with military advisors discussing a possible conquest of Britannia. They had been full of praise for his plans and they declared amongst themselves: Truly he is a son of '*Germanicus*'. Caligula's father '*Germanicus*' had been a renowned soldier and general. A hero of Rome. Caligula's reign had started well but his personality had changed following an illness and he had grown paranoid about his personal safety, eliminating those he considered a threat. He wasn't the man his father was and his people were beginning to realise that.

Iasonas whose name meant a healer stemmed from Ancient Greece and although he didn't know it, he was a direct descendant of Nabu. It was the way astrology had spread, first to Greece and then to other lands. The face of the Greek was burnished brown by the sun with thick eyebrows and light blue eyes.

Caligula acknowledged the entrance bow of the Greek seer and waved his hands in an expansive gesture which meant help yourself. Seats, food, drinks. "So," Caligula parried, "why the sudden urgency? What bad news have you to impart concerning Rome?"

The opening words of Iasonas were startling. "Rome will fall if Christianity isn't checked."

Caligula laughed, and so did his courtiers and palace people. The laughter petered out when he saw that Iasonas remained impassive with no hint of a smile.

"Lighten up, Iasonas," Caligula ordered. "What makes you think this about Rome?"

"I have seen it written in the stars."

This time there wasn't much laughter. The people could be a superstitious lot, even the emperor. Iasonas was a well-known seer whose predictions had borne fruit before. There were many in Rome who were afraid of him.

Caligula saw the unease in the faces of his people and moved to pacify them. He addressed his next words to the Greek: "What would you have me do, Iosanas? What should I do about this threat?"

Iosanas didn't respond immediately. Caligula tapped his foot impatiently. Eventually he said: "You must send out an emissary, perhaps a Vigilis, to investigate this new religion and to examine ways it can be stopped."

"A Vigilis?"

"Yes, emperor," Iosanas urged, "without delay."

Iosanas retired.

Caligula's face was creased in a frown as he watched Iosanas retreat from the room. He wanted to call him back. He wanted the Greek to put forward more suggestions, more names, more ideas. The emperor turned to his emissaries. "A Vigilis?" the man said, "well, do any of you have any ideas?"

A man called Faunus spoke up. "I know one such man, Emperor." Faunus was one of those individuals who was always trailing around behind the emperor. His beard and his cadaverous look gave him the appearance of a rabid Rabbi.

"His name?" Imperious tones.

"Marc Procus, emperor," Faunus replied.

Caligula was surprised that he knew the name. Hadn't the Senate appointed the man last year to re-examine the case of Julius Caesar? Rome would never stop looking into the circumstances surrounding the death of such a popular and dynamic leader. Even after eighty-one years. The passage of time might even shed further light on the mysteries of the case.

Caligula nodded slowly. "I know of this man," he remarked. "A Vigilis, indeed."

"Is he not otherwise engaged?" Juno asked, thinking of the brief the Senate had handed down last year. Juno was a bear of a man who was known throughout Rome and beyond as

Caligula's right-hand man. He was the type of individual who knew everyone of note and his influence was immense.

"Summon him," Caligula ordered. " If the Senate kicks up, refer them to me."

Caligula then washed his hands in a bowl of water. There could be no further discussion. The matter was settled.

Over!

THE SENATE COULD BE a powerful lobby of men that look acted as an advisory body between the emperor and the people. Upon hearing of Caligula's summons to Procus they were rightly annoyed. Procus couldn't be spared. He was carrying out important work for Rome, work they regarded as of the highest importance. There were always new developments with the passage of time that could shed light on a decades-old mystery and crime. It was never too late for justice and retribution should a guilty party emerge. Rome was good at retribution - crucifixions, death in the arena or food for hungry lions.

Three Senators ruled the roost: the undoubted leader of the bunch Antonia Minor with his hulking features, prominent nose and imperial looks. The Senator was a heavy man with big shoulders and big hands. The second man in this bunch was known by the name of Victoria and he carried himself with a military bearing, tall, ramrod straight. The third individual was known by the name Enna Calogero and he was the elder of the three and a Sicilian, the other two hailed from Rome. Calogero was also the wealthiest of the three because he had extensive vineyards in the south. They called him Calo for short. He was probably the fittest of the three because he was always outdoors and atop magnificent horses, including the Sanfratellano, indigenous to that area of Sicily.

Their women contributed equally too. Drusilla was the eldest of the three with her flame-coloured hair and was married to Antonia Minor; Giulea's small oval face and the strongest of the three was Calogero's wife, and Livia with her dark, Mediterranean looks was married to Victoria.

"So," Drusilla mocked, mockery being part of her nature, " you're going to allow Caligula walk all over you and snatch Procus from under your noses?"

"We're convening a meeting of the Senate to discuss these issues," Antonia Minor explained, shooting an annoyed look at his wife which she completely ignored. " Fat lot of good that will do you," she mocked. "Fat lot of good."

"He's the emperor," Calogero argued, plaintively. "What can we do?"

"Be men," Drusilla mocked. "Stand up to Caligula."

"He's too powerful," Giulea remarked, deciding to stand up for her man. "And so is Juno, his right-hand man."

"Ah, yes," Drusilla mocked. "Juno, Juno, Juno!"

Victoria had the greatest insight. "The Senate has always been sub-ordinate to the emperor," he observed, shrewdly. "It has always been that way." A red-purple stripe on his toga indicated he was a man to be reckoned with.

"You could set up a Curia Julia," Livia pointed out. They remained silent, thinking. On the face of it her suggestion had merit. The Curia Julia meetings every month were a good way to air grievances but it also meant going on the record and showing open opposition to the emperor. It was not how they liked to do business.

Antonia Minor pursed his lips and joined his fingers and hands like a man in prayer. A decision had formed in his mahogany brown eyes. "This Julius Caesar thing can wait. We can release the Vigilis from his contract and renew it when he returns. I think that would be best going forward. All in favour."

Five hands went up.

Antonia Minor gave Drusilla a stern look.

Slowly, she relented, and her hand rose.

Six hands.

"That's settled then," Antonia Minor declared. "Six hands is better than five."

CHAPTER 2.

The man known as Marc Procus swept aside the legal scrolls he had been leafing through, a pensive look on his inquisitive face, as he considered the brutal actions of Brutus in the slaying of Julius Caesar some eighty-one years before. He liked examining old cases; they could provide a mirror image of future events. He took an apple from a nearby Greek bowl and bit deep into it, chewing thoughtfully. Procus was renowned as a sort of ancient detective - a Vigilis.

The Latin meaning of the word 'Vigilis' meant to be alert, to be watchful and to be vigilant and Marc Procus at thirty-four years of age was all of those things. He had a military background and so had seen the worst of times as well as the best of times. He was a big man with round, broad shoulders and he had what could best be described as a commanding presence. He was dressed conservatively in a white gallibaya, military style boots, and a colourful keffiyeh. A bright blue one.

He gave a *'denarii'* to the boy who arrived to tell him that the emperor had summoned him. He told the boy to let the emperor know he'd be along shortly. Without ado, he unhurriedly shaved, washed and dressed and drank some water before leaving his house.

He moved easily through the streets, his chive green eyes missing nothing. Rome was a busy place. People were everywhere and hawkers used every scrap of ground to try and sell their wares. The smell of food cling to the hot, fetid air. Chicken skewers, goat, snails and salted peas were just some of the delicacies on offer. Dogs moved about freely, often at the feet of their owners. In the shadows, rats moved.

Fruit and vegetables were also widely available.

He was admitted to the emperor's quarters without preamble.

"You're late," Juno snapped at him.

"Sorry," he replied mildly.

Juno changed tack, seeing he couldn't bully this man. "What's happening with your investigation into Julius Caesar?"

Procus shrugged. "Trail's a cold one. I've seen nothing new. My full report will go before the Senate when it is ready. They appointed me."

It was an affront. Juno's face flushed bright red. "The Senate answers to the emperor," he growled in anger.

There was a long silence.

Sensing the tension in the room Caligula moved to dissipate it. He put his question direct to the Vigilis. "What do you know about Jesus of Nazareth, Procus?" he asked.

Procus shrugged his shoulders. "Next to nothing," he replied. "Who is he?"

"Who was he?" Caligula corrected. "To the Jews he was their king, to Christians he's their Messiah, and to the Romans he appeared to be a dangerous usurper who was crucified in Jerusalem."

"And when was this crucifixion?"

"Ten years ago," Juno put in, deciding to re-engage.

Another cold case, Procus thought.

"They say he was resurrected, this Jesus."

Procus looked at Juno's face suspecting merriment but the man's face remained serious.

Caligula spread his hands and remarked: "A movement has sprung up in this man's name, a Christian movement. We're charging you with finding out everything you can about this new movement, in particular, do they have ideas about taking Rome."

"Taking Rome?" He held down the laughter.

"That's what our seers are warning us about," Caligula warned.

Sorcerers in other words, Procus thought sourly.

Juno spoke up again. "The Procurator at the time in Jerusalem felt that Jesus deserved death, so it might be as well to start with him."

"What's the name of this procurator?"

"Pontius Pilate."

The name meant nothing to the Vigilis. Rome had many such characters on its books. He said as much.

"We believe he may have retired to Antioch," Caligula pointed out. That made sense. Rome would keep tabs on such a powerful figure, making sure he stayed out of trouble.

The Roman authorities knew about Pilate's struggles with the Jews in Jerusalem. Common knowledge.

Caligula washed his hands, his mind made up. "You'll leave for the port of Ostia tomorrow night where a ship awaits to take you east."

Procus left with his new commission. He didn't argue the point. He would leave that to the Senate.

"TOMORROW NIGHT?" LUNA complained. "How long will you be gone for?"

"A number of months, seven or eight maybe. Perhaps up to a year."

"Oh, Marcus, how am I going to get by without you?" she beseeched. She was slightly younger than her husband with bright blue inquisitive eyes and a complexion as pale as ebony marble. Her features were quite beautiful and her torso was slim despite having giving birth to twins four years ago. A boy and a girl. Calus and Cala.

They retired for the night, aware that this would be their last night together for quite some time. They made the most of it.

THE ROLLING MOTION of the ship was making Procus feel ill and he moved to his cabin to lie down. The thing he hated about sea sickness was that there was nowhere to go. One was stuck with it. He could hear the creaking of the ship - the ropes, the sails, the wooden hull.

Sleep eventually overcame him and the sickness subsided. A calmer sea greeted him the following morning and the master of the ship gave him a wide smile. He was a big man, with a long sword by his side, almost like that of a pirate. "Feeling better?" he queried.

"Much," Procus replied. He helped himself to a jug of water, icy cold, from a nearby barrel.

He looked around. The expanse of sea was a deep green colour. The ship he stood on was a grain boat, manned by a small army of oarsmen and seamen, complete with capstans and windlasses, about 180 feet long and a quarter of that in width. It was fifty feet in depth and cabins were located at the stern. The prow swept upwards gently from the curved stern and the mast held a huge red topsail. The master of the ship controlled the large rudder with his seasoned hands. He put a question to the master. "Where are we?"

"We've just rounded the toe of Italy," he replied. "We're making good headway. The winds have been good to us." He knew Italy lay off the port side and Sicily off the starboard although neither was visible because of a sea fog.

"We're making about eight knots an hour," the master explained, moving the rudder with his hands. "We should be in Crete in three days."

"Crete?"

"Our first port of call, Greece. We'll be there two days before continuing our journey."

A frown appeared on the features of Procus. He wondered did Rome know of these delays to his passage? They had impressed upon him the urgency of this investigation before he left. Still, he wasn't the master of the Punic. Doubtless the master, whose name he had discovered was Luca Alessandro, had his own orders.

Alessandro caught the look on the face of Procus and deduced the reason. He smiled apologetically. "Sorry," he commiserated. "Orders."

CRETE WAS HOT AND SUNNY.

The thing that bothered Procus about his current mission was having to make reports on people that as far as he could see were living good, solid lives. They weren't Zealots intent on bringing Rome down. Many of them had a faith that he envied.

He was a man without faith himself and yet when he looked around him at the beauty of the world - the deep blue sea and mirroring sky, the stars at night, the sounds and sights of nature - he had to admit, if only to himself, that there had to be something else. A creator, a God.

He wasn't one who believed in such gods as Mars or Diana, like the majority of his Roman counterparts. He was careful to keep such thoughts to himself. Rome had too many 'eyes' and 'ears'.

In Crete, he stood out as a visitor. It wasn't long before he was invited to a meal that evening with one of the chiefs - folk liked to hear from strangers what was happening in the world. It was a time of stories. The chief of the village introduced himself as Eirini and his wife as Eleni. They had two children who were watched over by Minas, a woman of indeterminate age with a magical smile and who helped Procus to find a seat. It was madness but it was a happy madness that somehow worked. It was from Eirini that he learned that the secret symbol of Christianity was the fish. Eirini carved it on the floor of the cottage and laughed at the expression of surprise on the Roman's face.

Their meal was a typical Greek one - cucumbers and olives, feta cheese, bread, and olive oil. A white wine accompanied it. Eirini began by describing the birth of Jesus and of how he began his mission at about thirty years of age. Any gaps in Eirini's knowledge were provided by Eleni who spoke with a soft Greek accent in contrast to the gruff tones of her husband.

Procus had a knowledge of Greek and in fact his command of languages helped him in his role as a Vigilis. As well as Greek, he spoke Latin, Aramaic, the languages of Hispania and Gaul, and even some German.

He was astonished by the miracles of Jesus - walking on water, feeding the multitudes, and raising the dead. He found himself believing this simple tale and for the first time in his life he felt a stirring within as the first faint elements of a faith stirred within him. It left him feeling confused.

He looked to where the two children played a card game in the corner of the house, watched over by Minas. Minas reminded him of his old grandma on his father's side, always there, always vigilant, until her untimely death from the kick of a horse. It was probably her influence that gave him his adventurous streak.

He didn't know where his suspicious streak came from. That seemed alien to him; something he'd like to throw aside like a cloak. It had become part of him when he was a teenager when he witnessed firsthand how underhand man could be. And women. Only in children could he see a sweet innocence.

The heat of the day was beginning to dissipate as evening closed in. He accepted the offer to stay the night, sending word back to the ship of his intention.

The Punic acknowledged, confirming it was in port for the night. They did inform him to be back by first light.

High overhead the stars twinkled.

THE PUNIC SAILED AT first light.

Shouts and orders intermingled as the sailors worked feverishly. Some men ate as they worked whilst others took a few minutes to grab some breakfast, normally a small dish known as *'jentaculum'*. The Roman diet was a rich one; fruit like grapes, figs, cereals and dried fruits. Some enjoyed cheeses and eggs with salted bread and perhaps even a drop of wine. Others drank milk and water. Some men lay on their stomachs as they ate believing that horizontal positioning aided digestion. A few, as soon as they had eaten, washed themselves using buckets of water and even cleaning their teeth using frayed sticks and dubious looking powders, the powders consisting of a mixture of ground-up hooves, eggshells and seashells, pumice, and ashes. One man grinned at Procus. "Gives us a healthier smile," he observed wryly.

Procus grinned at the man. Who was he to argue?

All over the ship, men were busy.

Their next port of call was Cyprus.

CYPRUS WAS HOT.

A part of Alexander the Great's empire in 333 BC, the island of Cyprus had been annexed in Rome in 58 BC. It became an important outpost of the Eastern Roman Empire and a significant trading post.

They would anchor in Kiteon in Cyprus.

Michalis had just tied up his boat when he came across Procus. " Just get here?" he queried.

Procus nodded. " Know any good inns for food?" he replied.

The fisherman smiled. "I do, if you don't mind home cooking."

"The best kind," Procus agreed. "Marc Procus!"

The fisherman took his hand. "Michalis Viachos."

Marc watched as the burly fisherman expertly took a sharp knife to the sword of the fish which he removed with one cut. The remainder of the fish was hoisted onto his broad shoulders. He swept aside the offers of Marc to assist.

Once again, Marc Procus, was given a Christian welcome in Cyprus, the people having a tendency to invite strangers into their homes so that they could learn what was happening in other lands. It proved a good way of catching up on the news of the day.

Androula expressed surprise to hear that some Roman women were adopting fashions from Gaul. "Oh, my," she exclaimed, in delight.

The deep blue eyes of Michalis rolled in his head and a ghost of a smile hit the chive green eyes of the Vigilis. He was invited to stay for dinner which consisted of swordfish, something the Vigilis hadn't tried before mostly because it was banned in Rome. Dolphins were banned too. There was also baked bread on the table, olives and various cheeses. There were also wild greens unique to Cypress that were eaten with olive oil and lemon dressing. Water had been drawn from a well outside and had been put into Greek urns of various shapes and sizes. Michalis had even discovered some wine for their guest.

They were very like Eirini and Eleni in their outlook on life although there were some differences: Eirini had been a chief and had been in a position to hire a slave girl - Minas. Michalis had told him earlier he made his living from the sea which explained how he could have such delicacies as swordfish for dinner. The swordfish came wrapped in an edible seaweed and local vegetables. The two children, Christos and Maria, tucked in.

"Christos?" the Vigilis asked softly, "is he named after the Christ?"

The face of Michalis hardened. "You know of these teachings?" he queried, suspicion in his tones. "You, a Roman?"

"The word spreads," the Vigilis explained and moved to placate the man, the gathering. "I mean you no harm."

Michalis seemed to visibly relax. "There are many who do not like these new teachings."

Procus nodded. "I understand."

Androula clapped her hands. "Enough of this silly talk," she exclaimed, and the children brightened. " Does anybody know any songs? Perhaps our guest?"

The sound of music filled the night air.

Procus had received word to report back at first light.

The Punic would sail then on her last leg.

CHAPTER 3.

Antioch was a bustling city standing at a point where the eastern end of the Roman Empire met Asia. It was here that Procus had gotten word that Pilate was in residence. The former procurator no longer held a position of power and had been recalled to Rome in 36 AD. to answer charges over a massacre of unarmed Arabs, including another self-proclaimed Messiah.

Delayed getting there, Tiberius was dead by the time he got there and representatives of the new emperor Caligula advised him to retire quietly. Exiled him, in fact. Pilate heeded their counsel and headed east again. New emperors normally dismissed the legal cases of their predecessors because they'd soon have enough headaches of their own.

It was ten years since the crucifixion of Jesus in Jerusalem and it was a death, he'd never been fully able to put out of his mind. He wished he had heeded his wife, Claudia. Her dreams had told her that Jesus was a righteous man but her advice to her husband on the matter had fallen on deaf ears.

Procus had stepped ashore at the Roman port of Seleucia Pieria and into a waiting carriage. He would be taken first to his inn where he could rejuvenate after his long sea journey.

The inn was a white sun-bleached dwelling, bright in the sunlight outside, cool and dark within. Palm trees fluttered in the slight sea breeze. The innkeeper greeted his guest, waving his hands and arms like a maniac, a grin etched to his thin features. He snapped his fingers and a woman appeared. "Marian will show you to your room."

The room was at the back, well away from any noise at the front. As the woman used a key to swing open the heavy wooden door, a boy squeezed past cradling a basin of cold water that had been drawn from a well. As soon as was alone, Procus removed his upper garments and splashed water onto his face. He then sat on the edge of the bed and removed his boots. He swung his legs up onto the bed and allowed his body to relax. His thoughts swung to Luna, his wife, who ran their home in Rome and who hadn't been exactly ecstatic last week when he had explained to her that the emperor had summoned him for a task abroad.

"How long will you be gone?" she had snapped.

He had shrugged. "Two months maybe."

"Two months? Did the Senate not have something to say about that."

He had shrugged again. "They're not happy," he explained, "but there isn't much they can do about it. They're up against the emperor."

A MAN CALLED JANUS bade him enter. He was a warrior type figure, short and squat, but tough as nails Procus was willing to bet. The man's hazel eyes were cold and pitiless, empty almost and hid a brain that was clever and quick thinking.

Pilate had slightly aquiline features, the cheeks of his face sunken and lines on his broad forehead. His expression could be indifferent, cruel. His hair was combed backwards, away from the thin featured looks, the nose slightly at odds with the remainder of the countenance, large slightly sunken eyes. He nodded to Procus as the Roman entered his dwelling, no friendship or warmth in the frigid features. One could tell he had been a man of power; it shone from him like a ray of blinding light.

Procus didn't waste any time on small talk.

"I'm here about Jesus."

"Who?"

"Jesus," Procus repeated. " You can't have forgotten the man. You had him crucified in Jerusalem ten years ago."

Pilate nodded his head slowly. "Ecce homo!" he said, softly. "The King of the Jews."

"So, you do remember?"

"I remember. His followers claimed he rose from the dead. It was the Sanhedrin who wanted him dead. I washed my hands of it."

"Easy way out?" Procus accused.

Pilate was suddenly angry. "I gave them a choice," he said. "A chance to save their prophet, their king.

Jesus. Or Barabbas."

"The latter a known enemy of Rome."

"It was the people's choice," Pilate said, plaintively. " What is it with this Jesus?" he demanded, angrily. "Ten years have passed since his crucifixion and I'm still haunted by the events."

"Guilty conscience, perhaps?"

Pilate said nothing. He still looked angry. " I did my job," he eventually pleaded. "I did my duty."

Procus had heard enough and his voice was cold as he addressed the former procurator.

"Pilate, I'll be putting in a report on this whole issue and from the sound of things your name will feature prominently. I'd use the next few weeks to prepare yourself. Rome will ask some hard, tough questions."

A long silence ensued after Procus had left the room, and Pilate turned questioning eyes on Janus, his assistant.

"Who does he think he is?" Pilate queried. "I could quash him under my boot."

"He's not without certain influence," Janus pointed out. "In Rome."

"With Caligula?" Pilate scolded scornfully. "He's no Tiberius."

"Or Augustus," Janus added, showing his age as he could remember events back that far. He was a thin, ascetic individual with white, grey hair.

"Quite," Pilate agreed. He looked at Janus. "Send Sicarii in to see me."

Janus quickly bowed and left the room.

THE MAN SUMMONED BY Pontius Pilate looked brutish in appearance. No more than twenty-five, the man had a long scar running along his right cheek. He was neither too old nor too young and he listened attentively as Pilate announced what he wanted done. He had slunk into the room like a dark shadow, light on his feet, his voice light with tension.

The man who had given him the scar was dead. He had killed him in the gladiator arena. He had won his freedom when Pilate had seen firsthand his courage and his daring.

"I'm worried about this Procus individual. Follow him, and report back on everyone he meets."

"Do you want him to have an accident?"

Pilate was reflective, before responding: "It might come to that, but not yet. For the moment, just follow him. We don't want anything untoward happening to him just yet. Rome would look at that with great disfavour."

"They might throw you to the lions," the Sicarii joked. He had a penchant for dark humour.

Pilate laughed darkly. "They might," he agreed. "They just might at that."

CHAPTER 4.

Sipping a ca'lida at his inn on the morning following his meeting with Pontius Pilate, Marc Procus had become aware that he was been followed. A ca'lida was a warm drink favoured particularly by the Romans and the Greeks and consisted of warm water mixed with wine and spices. His also had a squeeze of lemon juice and a spoonful of honey. He watched the man surreptitiously, taking note of every detail. It didn't take a genius to figure out who was behind the surveillance - Pilate.

Having slept on the problem he had decided overnight to submit a report on Pilate and to send it back with the ship he had arrived on which was in port for another few days. The Punic had orders to return with silk and spices.

Taking no more note of the man watching him, Procus retreated to his room. He spent the next hour writing away at his desk.

The sun was still shining as he re-emerged from his inn. The man known as Sicarii was still standing in the shadows and Procus noticed the stranger falling in behind him as he moved through the streets. His brain had been working on the problem whilst he was writing and it didn't take a mathematician to figure out that the man worked for Pontius

Pilate. He had, after all, only appeared after his conversation with the former procurator.

Procus began some evasive manoeuvres - increasing his pace, ducking in and out of markets, trying to disappear into the crowds. The man still clung to him.

The lips of Procus thinned. He was dealing with a professional. A different approach would be needed.

He ducked into a nearby alley and moved behind a door. He heard the heavy breathing of the man and as the man started to turn, Procus slammed the door into him. Winded, the man staggered back. Procus stepped behind him his right a blur as it rose and fell, the palm of his hand hitting the Pilate man on the nape of the neck and knocking him out, cold.

Procus moved off without a backwards glance.

To the casual observer, the violence was sudden and shocking but there was a hint of a smile on the Roman's face as he moved off.

He moved more briskly now, making directly for the port. It looked different in daylight. The water had an azure quality that looked like the lakes of heaven. The boats were colourful, different colours merging and fishermen were busy with their nets. Sails were equally colourful.

The Punic was still in the same place it had docked at the other night, heavy ropes tied to pontoons on the docks. There was a smell of fish on the warm air and the heady smell of seawater and washed-up kelp. The gentle lapping of waves could be heard.

"Permission to board," Procus called out.

"Permission granted."

As he walked up a gangway, the lips of Procus thinned as he observed the Sicarii weaving into sight, the rapid recovery of the man surprising him. The man had made a lucky guess of his intended destination. The man glared at Procus. If looks could have killed?

THE CAPTAIN OF THE Punic fingered the scroll thoughtfully. "So," he decided, "you want this delivered into the hands of Caligula and you're proceeding with your mission."

Procus nodded. "They'll know that without being told but tell them anyway."

The captain grinned, and Procus grinned with him. "Don't keep them in the dark," he remarked. Men were busy, loading supplies onto the Punic. She would sail that very night back to Ostia with stops in Athens and Malta.

As Marc left by the gangway, Sicarii watched his every move, hidden in the shadows. Some knew it as Panormus, others as Palermo, but to the Sicarii it was always home. It was here in the back alleys of Palermo near the port that he had spent his formative years. He could trace his lineage back to the ancient Sicani people, also known as Sicanians. From an early age he had been involved in thievery and it was from an early age that he had learned how to use weapons. At first knives, then later the garrotte.

He had also learned how to shadow people without being seen himself.

All in all, he was a man to be feared.

CHAPTER 5.

Trade in the Mediterranean had been flowing since the third millennium BCE - the Roman Empire would rise in the first millennium BCE. Under the Phoenicians, trade flourished especially as the Phoenicians were expert boat builders. Ports and harbours were established in many different lands to encourage inter-trading. It was a 'win win' for everyone.

The old Silk Road was a major trading route with the countries of the Far East sending silks, spices and other exotic goods.

There was talk that Jesus himself had travelled the Silk route, a route that would take in Persia, Afghanistan and India. Ancient Indian scrolls would tell of Issa, a great prophet and holy man from Palestine who lived and preached among the people and who preached in the great temples with the Shamans.

However, the Vigilis dismissed such talk, preferring to concentrate his energies on the last three years of the life of Jesus. He wanted to get his reports done and go back to his beloved Juna and children as soon as possible. To believe that to follow Jesus and his path would see him traipsing through Persia, Afghanistan and India would be an arduous undertaking and would add two years, at least, to the work. He had no intention of being gone that long.

NOBODY KNEW HOW THE fire started but because the boat was mostly made of wood it quickly caught hold and consumed everything in its path. Flame licked into every corner of the ship and caught the huge topsail resulting in a huge fireball. Men screamed in terror of their lives and more than one jumped overboard and tried to swim for it. Unfortunately, the ship was just too far from shore and the currents of the Mediterranean too treacherous for many to survive. At this time of the year the waters were at their coldest and men found that the water was every bit as dangerous as the fire; in fact, it was deadlier.

Orange flames leapt across the night sky. That was another thing; the closing darkness. And suddenly as though things weren't bad enough there was a blood-curdling scream that chilled every man to the bone as one sailor was caught in the jaws of a sea dog. A monstrous shark.

On the mainland there was confusion and panicked shouts as men tried to organise a rescue operation.

"A ship afire," someone shouted. "The Punic."

"Break out the boats," someone else shouted.

From across the water, they could hear the horrible crackling and the screams of terror. The ship was mostly made of wood which helped to fuel the fire further. It burned for a good two hours before a deathly silence took hold, a silence that stretched to the mainland. It had now become a recovery operation rather than a rescue. Anyone in the sea would long have perished from hypothermia. Others had drowned and a few had been taken by sea dogs, less said the better.

The stars overhead still glowed brightly, unwittingly witnesses to the tragedy unfolding below. The moon too was there, unblinking. The waters were calm again, black in the darkness.

Everything was charred, burnt black.

And then, there was a huge sizzling sound as the dark waters of the Mediterranean claimed the Punic, dragging the ship down to a watery grave.

And then everything was still.

The Sicarii from his vantage point on the rocky shoreline moved away.

MARC PROCUS HAD LEFT Antioch that afternoon and so he didn't learn for a number of months the fate of the Punic.

He had joined a caravan, the safest way to travel overland on long journeys and a safety net against brigands, wild animals and other hazards that travelling cross-country brought. There was safety in numbers.

The caravan moved south with Jerusalem as its destination. The journey was three hundred miles and averaging about twenty miles a day would take about fifteen days. Donkeys helped in transporting some of the heavier goods.

At night they stopped and broke out the tents. They often had a central area where a fire would be lit and people would exchange gossip and stories and sing songs. If lucky, sometimes a poet might be along and would recite some verses.

Procus had teamed up with a family who needed help with their animals.

It could be slow-going but every step took them closer to their destination.

Jerusalem beckoned!

CHAPTER 6.

About thirteen days had passed since the Vigilis had departed Ostia near Rome bound for Antioch and new news had reached the ears of Juno from the port concerning the return of the big grain ship - the Punic. The ship was lost, sunk after a disastrous fire. Only one man had lived to tell the tale and from what Juno could gather he was already on his way back to Rome on another ship. Juno arranged to have the ship met immediately upon its return and have the survivor questioned.

Caligula agreed to meet him immediately and Juno wasted no time in informing him of the loss.

"This survivor," Caligula announced, "he will be questioned on his return?"

"The wheels are in motion, Emperor."

"When can we expect his return?" It was a Monday.

"Next Saturday, Emperor."

"And no word yet from Procus?"

"Not yet. We estimate that he must have met Pontius Pilate by this stage and continued with his investigation, wherever that led him. Perhaps he submitted a report with the ship that brought him out. Who knows?"

"So, we've no choice but to wait and see," Caligula finalised. "If Procus submitted a report with the ship that is now lost, burnt to a cinder."

Juno could only wring his hands in agreement. The meeting ended on a sour note, Caligula dismissing him with a flaccid wave of his pale hand.

He didn't say what was on his mind to the emperor. If Procus had indeed submitted an early report, something he had been encouraged to do before he left, then he might not know that his communications had not reached Rome and it might be some time before they heard from him. He concluded it was best to leave Caligula in the dark on that one. The man would figure it out for himself in time.

Juno saw no reason to antagonise the man. He knew when to keep his mouth shut.

He decided to send for Faunus.

The rabid rabbi wandered in. "Faunus, I have a job for you," Juno began.

Dirty work!

FAUNUS TRIED TO KEEP a low profile by booking a small room in a little village close to Calogero's residence, but it wasn't long before his presence was reported to the big man himself. Calogero was no fool and he knew Juno suspected him of plotting against the emperor.

He heard Faunus had been asking questions. Pointed questions, pertinent questions. About him! Who were his visitors? How frequently did they visit? How long did they stay?

The man was trying to build up a case. However, he was as operating in an environment and a country he didn't understand.

However, this was Sicily, and Sicilian blood ran deep.

Calo had heard about the return of a man from further east, a man versed in their ways.

Calo sent for the Sicarii.

A paid assassin.

THE SICARII KNEW HIS game well.

He didn't make any immediate moves against Faunus allowing the man free rein, or seemingly so, but in reality, Faunus was being watched around the clock.

Everything about the man was noted: his rabid looks and gaunt features, his style of clothing, boots, tunic, belts. Personality traits were noted: what time he retired at night, when would he be at his lowest ebb, the best time of the day to take him.

Nothing was left to chance.

The Sicarii decided to move against him in person because Faunus at times exhibited a dangerous air. He'd bring two or three men to help get rid of the body and they had already decided that would have to be at sea, weighed down with chains.

They knew by the time it would take that they would probably know more about Faunus than the man knew himself.

They were that ready.

CHAPTER 7.

In the ten years since the crucifixion Jerusalem hadn't changed much. It was still a city that Jews flocked to, and as in the time of Jesus, the city was filled with Pharisees, rabbis, shepherds, traders and everything in between.

Procus had never been to Jerusalem before and he looked around with interest. The people he noted looked affluent enough. He could see some bathing in the waters of Siloam prior to entering the temple. The pool was on the southern slope of the Wadi Hilweh, or so his guide told him. He had decided to appoint a guide for this part of his journey, a man by the name of Yaakov, which Procus understood to translate to Jacob, and the seventy something man had the dark, somber looks of a Galilean.

He told the guide to bring him to the Roman commander of the region. The Roman commander looked a bit perplexed at his presence and remarked that they had no word of his eminent arrival.

Procus frowned.

That was most unusual of Rome, he thought. He would have imagined that fresh orders or instructions would have been awaiting him in Jerusalem. Did they think he was psychic?

Procus felt annoyance rising within him and he struggled to keep his voice level.

There was nothing to do but give the commander his address and wait for Rome to get in touch. In the meantime, his investigation into the Christian community could begin.

He had already submitted a report on those he had met thus far but he had emphasised that they were simple people with no designs on Rome. He had begun compiling a list of names of those he wished to see in Jerusalem.

Following a good night's sleep in an inn he had found and following a tasty breakfast he left his quarters to explore what Jerusalem had to offer.

He decided to take a walk amongst the narrow alleyways that made up Jerusalem. There was no better way to get a grip on the city.

He walked the Via Dolarosa. He saw the stone marked 'Ecce homo' - Behold the Man. The stone underfoot was uneven, unhewn. Rough. The way of sorrow began at the Antonia Fortress to the Church of the Holy Sepulchre. The route began more or less from the Lion's gate near the Antonia Fortress.

In his mind's eye he could almost see the baying crowd, Jesus falling and receiving help from Simon the Cypriot, the crying women, and the savage, implacable Roman faces devoid of pity, devoid of mercy. The claustrophobic nature of the narrow alleyways was overwhelming. He breathed deeply. He could smell a spice in the hot air, saffron perhaps? Market stalls were everywhere. There was noise everywhere. And the stone beneath his sandals were still rough, still unhewn.

The summer sun blasted out of the heavens.

HE SAW THE PLACE OF execution. What was it they called the place? Golgotha. Calvary in Latin. Known locally as Skull Hill.

He retraced his footsteps, pausing for a rest near the Damascus Gate. He sipped some water, using a small Greek urn, the urn itself devised for such a purpose. The sun blasted down on Jerusalem like a hot furnace, no pity in its countenance. Summer. The smell of olive trees. Wild garlic. Wild onions.

He had begun his journey in March and four months had passed in quick succession. July was just around the corner, a month he sometimes dreaded because of the heat.

"Interesting huh?" Yaakov burst into his thoughts. Yaakov was a wizened old man who still had a spring in his step and who made a good living showing people around the Holy City.

Procus enjoyed walking around strange cities and places. He found it was a great way to get to know a place. There was no sense of rush or urgency the way a horse or carriage might bring. One could indulge the senses.

Smell the flowers, or even the dung. Listen to the people and eye up the sights. Taste different foods, touch different silks in the colourful marketplaces. There was a cacophony of different sounds, different accents. Many people passed through Jerusalem because it lay on a trade route.

Procus kept moving, taking everything in.

Some of the scenes reminded him of how he had grown up in Rome, an only child. His father was often away on business, an administrator in the olive oil business. His mother used to do her own pottery and their house was full of clay pots and jugs and vessels of every type and she sold quite a few pieces including at a market stall every Saturday where Marc would often find himself helping out. He liked the markets; the colour and excitement, the sea of happy faces, the bustle and the noise.

It all reminded him of how he had grown up in Rome, an only child. His father was often away on business, an administrator in the olive oil business. His mother used to do her own pottery and their house was full of clay pots and jugs and vessels of every type and she sold quite a few pieces including at a market stall every Saturday where Marc would often find himself helping out. He liked the markets; the colour and excitement, the sea of happy faces, the bustle and the noise.

As an active young boy, Marc wasn't short of other children to play with. Games included marbles, tops, wooden swords, seesaws, kites, whips, chariots, swings and dolls although he mostly left the latter two to the girls of the group. He particularly liked a dice game known as knucklebones.

Romeu Minerva Quintus was his best friend, a boy of similar age and temperament who filled his head with stories of Roman conquests and fights, a boy whose father was a soldier. It gave Marcus a sense that he could do the same when he was of age to do so although from the age of eight to eleven there were early signs of his Vigilis thinking, moving out individuals from his group who were up to no good.

His friend Romeu hadn't lived to see him become a soldier, dying from an illness at the tender age of fifteen, the same year his father succumbed to the same virus. A year later, his mother was gone too. It wasn't long after those tumultuous events that he would meet Luna.

THE SICARII HAD LONG abandoned his task of watching over the Vigilis and had moved back to Sicily. Following Procus had proved burdensome - the man seemed to spend his time talking to all manner of folks - and seemed to spend copious amounts of time writing away in his room.

The Sicarii had heard about the recall of Pontius Pilate to Rome and his thin lips had curled coldly. He won't be back, he surmised. Men recalled to Rome in that way very rarely returned - they had dirtied their bib in some way and it was best to stay clear of such associations, lest one be found equally guilty by association.

The Sicarii laughed to himself. Pilate had at best been a meal ticket. He wasn't too worried. A man with his capabilities would always be in demand, especially in a treacherous place like Sicily.

It was nice to be home.

He was sipping some red wine when he received the word from Calogero.

He liked Calogero – the Senator often had interesting jobs.

Over the years, the Senator or his two companions, had dispatched some powerful men and enemies. Sometimes the body had to disappear and other times it needed to be found as a message. One such killing had such repercussions that the Sicarii himself had to flee Rome. He went east and that was how he met Pilate.

Now that he was back on home-ground he felt sure Calogero would have new work for him.

He liked keeping busy!

CHAPTER 8.

The survivor of the wrecked Roman ship, the Punic, stood trembling before the emperor Caligula, the expression on his thin, bony face that of a man expecting to be fed to the lions at any minute. Roman soldiers had taken him into custody as soon as his ship docked in Ostia and had bundled him unceremoniously into a horse led cart. They said little to him except to confirm that the emperor wished to see him.

The emperor? Wished to see him?

What about?

He soon found out. The emperor wanted to know about the man they had brought out to Antioch. It fell to Juno to question the man and seeing his fear he moved to put the man at ease. "You're not in trouble," he assured him. The questions concerned the man that had accompanied them to Antioch. The passenger. "Had he known him well? Had he spoken to him?"

He shook his head. "The man kept very much to himself. He spoke with the master of the ship a few times."

"What about?"

"Don't know," he replied, honestly. "I think he was a little sick that first night...the seas were choppy...he was a little seasick."

"What makes you think that?"

"Well, he retired very early to his cabin, wasn't seen much until the following morning. And one of the other men heard him retching and spoke about it."

"He disembarked at Antioch, right?"

"That's right."

"And you never saw him again after that?" the man called Juno queried.

The man hesitated.

Juno spotted the reticence immediately. "Well man?" he demanded. "Out with it."

"He returned to the ship before we sailed. Met with the master and handed him what looked liked scrolls."

A *report*.

So, Procus had put in a report? When would his next one come in? Juno wondered for the thousandth time.

Juno looked at the survivor again. "Did Procus give any indication of where he might be going afterwards?"

The survivor shook his head.

"You we're lucky," he observed, hiding his chagrin. "How did the fire start?"

"It started in the holds and took hold lightening fast. Some of the men were killed in the fire including the master but most drowned when they went overboard. A few were taken by sea dogs."

The survivor shuddered. " I grabbed a bit of wood and it took me ashore, more dead than alive."

"And you never saw Procus again?"

"No. Never."

Juno indicated the man could go.

They waited until he was out of sight and earshot and then Juno turned to his emperor. "Suppose," he conjectured, " that his report concerned Pilate and that the report was negative. Might Pilate have taken steps to prevent that report reaching us?"

"You mean he may have caused the fire in some way?"

"Precisely."

"Summon Pilate to Rome immediately."

"I've been thinking," Juno added, "about where the investigation of Procus might have taken him and we may be able to intercept him at some point."

"Where are you thinking of?"

"A few places - Ephesus, Jerusalem. Christianity is strong from those areas and it seems logical that Procus would want to go to the source."

"See to it at once, Juno. Send messengers out after him. Set up a proper chain of communications. We need to keep abreast of his findings."

THE FURORE SURROUNDING the sinking of the Punic surprised Pontius Pilate and reminded him of the uproar in Jerusalem when Jesus had been condemned. Emissaries had been sent back and forth with orders to leave no stone upturned in their quest for answers. Specialists had been sent in, experts in arson and they gathered every piece of boating that had floated ashore. A few even dived on the wreck although what they hoped to accomplish at ten fathoms was anybody's guess. Pilate shook his head at the folly of man.

He was amused by all this commotion he had created. The Sicarii had left, following the path of Procus in a second parallel caravan that mirrored the movement of the first. The Sicarii had signed on as a scout which gave him a certain freedom to roam and to scout the land via horseback.

It also allowed him to keep a close eye on Marc Procus.

The *Vigilis*.

CHAPTER 9.

Pontius Pilate summoned to appear before the emperor Caligula was a very different kettle of fish when compared with the quaking survivor and Juno noticed the arrogance of the man as he strode in to Caligula's quarters.

Juno didn't beat around the bush. "What do you know about the Punic?"

"The what?"

"The ship that carried Marc Procus to Antioch. Let's not play games, Pontius."

"Ah, Marc Procus?"

"You know the name, I take it?"

"He came to see me about a man I had crucified ten years ago in Jerusalem."

"Jesus of Nazareth?"

"Yes. The King of the Jews."

"And why was the man crucified?" Caligula queried, in his high-pitched tones.

"He was an enemy of Rome, Emperor. He declared himself to be a king - King of the Jews. We all know there can be only one Caesar."

The answer mollified the emperor but Juno wasn't so casually brushed aside. Encouraged by Faunus, he put question after question to Pontius Pilate.

44

The lips of Pilate curled as he observed his accusers. There was a time in life when such men as these would have quailed at his power; a time when he had the ear of Sejanus, who in turn had the ear of Tiberius. Pilate had been born into an elite equestrian family, similar to Sejanus who had Pilate recruited for the role of governor of Judea. No big deal.

His cruel lips pursed. He could once have made such men quail but those days were gone, lost in the mists of time. Emperors these days had none of the leadership qualities of their forefathers and were in the opinion of Pilate weak.

He wondered where the Sicarii was?

"WHAT WILL WE DO WITH him?" Caligula asked. "Juno?"

"Crucify him," Juno spat out. "Give him some of his own medicine."

Although not without its merits Caligula needed to tread cautiously. Pilate was still a man with influence and his family were well known. Caligula looked towards the rabid rabbi. "Faunus?"

"Exile, perhaps emperor," Faunus wheezed, his reedy voice lacking conviction. "Crucifixion wouldn't be warranted. He's still a Roman!"

On the face of it though exile might warrant a further look. Pilate could be moved out of the way to some backwater where he would be quickly forgotten. Caligula liked the sound of that. He asked an attendant to bring him a bowl of water and he washed his hands.

"Exile it will be," he decided. "Send him north. Gaul perhaps, or Switzerland. I never want to see him again."

Exile.

It was tantamount to a death sentence.

CHAPTER 10.

M arc Procus suddenly found himself summoned to the quarters of the Roman Governor and he breathed a sigh of relief because it seemed Rome had finally woken up and seemed about to give him new orders. He was taken aback when they accused him of not staying in touch.

"I submitted a report in Antioch," he insisted.

"It was never received," he was told.

It was then that he learned about the fate of the Punic that had brought him to Antioch.

"Fire?" he queried. "Sunk?"

"With most hands," the governor pointed out. "Rome wants you to submit a new report without delay. They've already summoned Pontius Pilate to answer questions about the fire."

"They think he was involved in some way?"

The governor grunted, remaining non-committal. In politics it paid to be guarded with your mouth.

Procus was glad he hadn't followed a political path in life. He had been raised in Rome for the most part but his father's duties as a Roman soldier saw them moving about quite a bit - Hispania, Malta, and Antioch. His mother hadn't been as keen on all of the travelling but she was dutiful to her husband's wishes.

Marc himself liked seeing how other cultures flourished. He remembered he had liked the liveliness of Hispania, the smiling people, the bull fighting, and the ceremonies. It was a country full of colour with nice practices like the siesta in the afternoons.

Malta on the other hand was a welcoming place complete with its own unique charm. A fishing island.

Returning to his quarters from the Roman garrison he picked up his writing instruments and prepared his report for Rome. He included details of his interactions with Christians in Crete and Cyprus and added his opinion that these people were to be left alone - they were the salt of the earth. He put his suspicions regarding Pilate onto paper and later that afternoon he returned to the garrison with his sealed report.

By nightfall the report would be on a ship bound for Rome. All roads led to there.

He went down the stairs to the supper room where he ordered a broth infused with basil, bread, olives and feta cheese. He drank some watered-down red wine with his meal. He ate some fruit - grapes, oranges, melons. He liked the food of Jerusalem.

Tomorrow, even though a Saturday would be a busy one. He had several interviews lined up and he hoped to have a clear understanding of Christianity by the time the new week rolled around.

His sleep that night was uneasy as though devils were playing around in his mind. He tossed and turned. In far off lands, events were occurring that would bring great change to his outlook on life.

But that was for the future.

HE DREAMED OF LUNA that night and of how they had first met. He had been a young soldier on leave but dressed in a uniform: a knee length and short sleeved tunic, the wool suit dyed red. His focale or scarf prevented his armour from chafing his neck, a leather baldric that supported his sword and a bronze helmet with a horsehair crest. He certainly looked the business and Luna was taken aback by his dashing appearance.

She, on the other hand, was wearing a simple yellow dress but he moved immediately to put her at ease by making her laugh. " You're dressed in wedding colours?" he queried with amusement.

She laughed. "Yes."

It was no open secret that girls getting married in Rome wore yellow as part of their costume. They spent the rest of the evening in conversation and he walked her to her home. Her parents were diplomats and often away from home and she had a brother who was also a soldier, stationed east somewhere.

He agreed to meet her again for a meal that included yellowfin tuna, vegetables, olives and legumes with white wine.

He next brought her to the games, but just the sports.

She didn't like blood sports, so he never brought her to those. She told him a funny story about some men too caught up in the emotion of it all, goading the people they had arrested and who were about to face the lions, but they were so preoccupied by hate that they failed to see the Roman guard withdraw and they got the fright of their lives when the wooden trap door opened behind them.

"Wait," they cried. "This isn't right."

Forced out into the arena they ran hurriedly towards the emperor and pleaded their case.

The emperor listened with amusement and his thumb stood poised - the four men in front barely breathing, afraid to look - and then the thumb went down.

Death!

An angry growl signalled that the lions were prowling. The four men tried to hide but there was nowhere to hide. Two of their number went down amid fur, teeth and blood.

Procus nodded with a tight grin. "Guess they got what they deserved."

The betrothal happened one year in, a ceremony that committed the couple to one another and where both families met one another. A dowry was paid over, gifts exchanged and everything was sealed with a kiss. The actual wedding occurred one year later.

When the children arrived within three years their marriage flourished and grew stronger.

CHAPTER 11.

S aturdays or Shabbat as the Jewish people called it marked the Sabbath and could be a testing time for visitors to Jerusalem unused to the ways of the people. It began on Friday afternoons and finished at sundown on the Saturday. At the start of Shabbat, religious Jews could be seen praying at the Wailing Wall. Procus had been invited to a Shabbat dinner, normally a festive family occasion, with a man called Peter. There was some confusion over the man's name, with some folk calling him Cephas. A Greek translation, it was explained to Procus. Nevertheless, he had been assured that Peter was the man to talk to if he wanted to understand Christianity. It was the understanding of Procus that Peter was one of the leaders of this new church.

The big fisherman from Galilee surprised him with his warm welcome. His wife also had a pleasant temperament and a warm smile. Procus noticed that the handshake of the fisherman was strong and firm. He was invited into the stone dwelling which seemed to have a number of rooms but the centre area was where guests were entertained. He accepted some water. And grapes.

"So," Peter began, "do you know anything about Christianity?"

"It's my understanding that you follow the path laid down by Jesus Christ and that he was put to death ten years ago by Pontius Pilate."

Peter's face clouded over. "Ah yes," he exclaimed softly, regret in his tones. "Pilate."

There was a world of meaning in that one word.

Peter continued to speak. "Some Ethiopians I spoke with recently seemed to think Pilate had turned over a new leaf and spoke very highly of his wife Probia."

Procus shook his head. "Pilate is out for only one thing...himself. I met him before coming here. There's been no change to the man; none that I could see anyway."

Peter accepted that with a sad shake of the head. "Gospels are been written as we speak which will highlight the life of Jesus and help give testimony to his teachings. Matthew's gospel, in particular, will shed some light on the nativity and the major events surrounding the birth of Jesus. His story will be more immediate than that of the other scribes; more heartwarming, more human."

He paused before adding softly: "did you know that men came to kill him when he was a baby. That despot King Herod learned that there was to be a new king of the Jews and he ordered, slain, all the newborns of Bethlehem up to the age of two. Jesus was saved by divine intervention, and his parents of course."

"Who were his parents?" Procus asked, picking up a few more grapes. Delicious. He had often noticed that fruit and vegetables had a better taste when grown locally.

"Joseph of Nazareth," he explained. "Gone now. And Mary, his mother. She lives in Ephesus now with our people there."

"Happily?"

Peter's face clouded for a moment. "As well as can be expected," he explained, "with her son gone, and her husband. Prayer helps her a lot and the Sacred Mass. It is expected she will return to her native land some day."

The Vigilis was silent, thinking.

Ephesus! It seemed like an important place.

He would go there.

It would mean another boat journey. That or two caravans north, roughly six hundred miles and taking over thirty days. Life was too short. He'd take a boat.

And afterwards back to Rome. It seemed that a visit to Ephesus would make his work complete.

Ephesus would be the decider.

After Ephesus, Rome.

The Eternal City.

CHAPTER 12.

S trangely enough Sundays were also a day of rest and prayer for the people who called themselves Christians, something Marc Procus found perplexing and baffling. The Jews themselves thought nothing of reopening their businesses and trading again. He was surprised to find out they were at prayer again; prayer seemed to be at the centre of everything they did, even now at breakfast. He noticed Peter and his wife refraining from food and they explained that fasting before Holy Communion was a necessary part of their faith. He felt humbled and guilty about eating, but Peter encouraged him to continue. "It would be a boring world if we all did the same thing."

Procus grinned in agreement. "It would," he observed.

He was starting to change his mind about these people. They were men and women of peace, not war. He could not see how they would become a threat to Rome, as Caligula, Juno, Faunus, and the rest of the entourage had insisted. He didn't like his role in all of this. The feeling that he was a spy in their midst, having to make reports back to his masters in Rome. It gave him an edgy feeling; a chill. A feeling that he was an outsider. A Judas. They had also hinted that his own family might have to pay a price if his mission failed.

PROCUS WAS FEELING edgy and he didn't know why.

Never before had his work put his family in any danger and he pondered what to do as a best option. He picked up a quill and decided to write to Senator Calogero. Calo had told him before leaving that if he needed any assistance with future happenings not to hesitate.

When night came, he was easier in mind. His communication was on the way to Calogero's palatial residence in Agrigento in Sicily. Agrigento itself was known for its ruins from the ancient city of Akragas in the Valley of the Temples.

It was a place Calogero had come across as a young man when he married his Sicilian bride.

Like many Sicilian women of her age, she possessed a raw, dark beauty that spoke of Mediterranean blood and Calogero had known after that first look that she was the one.

Calogero had been born just as Augustus was assuming power. Born Gaius Octavius in 63 BC, he had been adopted by the great Julius Caesar and by defeating Antony in 31 BC. his power was supreme, unconquerable.

He had been brought to the Senate floor as a young boy by his father who also belonged to the great assembly. He was told about the three controlling bodies - the plebeian council, the Tribal Assembly, and the Comitia Centuriata or Centuriate Assembly.

Caesar Augustus had managed to change virtually everything about Rome transferring the republic to an empire in the process and in effect becoming the first great Roman Emperor of Imperial Rome.

During his lifetime he improved the lot of Roman citizens in so many ways - marriage laws were strengthened, a proper fire and police brigade was set up, roads were improved and the Empire was expanded. Upon his death he was proclaimed by the Senate to be a Roman God.

Calogero had learned the rules of Rome well. He determined even as a young boy that he would tread these very stones and tiles and would follow quite literally in his father's considerable footsteps. Power was here, an invisible source he could almost taste, touch, feel.

They controlled political life, including military tribunals; they controlled the social fabric of society, and they governed through laws they had enacted.

WITH A NAME LIKE ANTONIA Minor, it didn't take a genius to figure out that his father would have been called Antonia Senior or simply Antonia but Antonia Minor was destined to lose his father at an early stage, bringing him under the direct rule of his grandfather who had worked for the great Julius Caesar. When one thought of Rome there were three distinct periods: from 753 BC-625 BC to 510 BC was known as the Period of Kings; the Republic of Rome from 510 BC to 31 BC; and imperialistic Rome from 31 BC to 476 AD.

Antonia Minor had excelled in school with a penchant for languages and history. He thought about teaching when he grew up but the cut and thrust of politics was to claim him. Both his mother and his grandfather had conspired to get him into politics.

Like everything in life, Antonia Minor, rose rapidly in the Senate becoming a prominent orator along the way. He was outspoken and his voice could be like a whiplash towards opponents. It would be fair to say he had as many enemies as friends on the Senate floor.

He'd often heard Rome was bloody, but he hadn't seen that side of it. He stayed away from gladiator games and the like, preferring a glass of wine and a good game of chess.

VICTORIA WAS UNDER no such illusions. Having seen his fair share of bloodshed he knew only too well the harsher side of Roman rule. He was the warrior of the trio having fought within Rome's legions. He had mostly fought in battles against German insurgents.

He was younger than the other two by about ten years, something which often brought amusement when they gathered.

He was speaking now to the other two in low tones. "It's my understanding that Caligula and his cronies…"

"Faunus and Juno," Antonia interrupted.

"That they questioned Pontius Pilate at length," Victoria resumed, ignoring the interruption, and speaking with animation. "Seemingly some vessel called The Punic which set sail with Marc Procus was set alight and communications with Procus broke down as a result. There was uproar and murder but they finally managed to restore communication."

"Crazy mission," Calogero added. "The sooner we have Procus back under our wing, the happier I'll be."

"Amen to that," said the other two in tandem. In unison.

CHAPTER 13.

They came ashore from Greek-type boats, loud and gruff, armour and swords at the ready. They marched inland.

They were Roman soldiers.

They sought out who they wanted from lists they had and put them to the sword.

Their ships were driven by oars and sails and the corvus or bridge had an iron spike which could be driven into the deck of an enemy ship, holding the bridge fast. The Roman galleys were better than their Greek counterparts because stronger wood, fir and oak, was used in their construction. Roman ships had come a long way since their war with the seafaring Carthaginians in 264 BC.

Screams broke out wherever the soldiers went. There were other screams too, the sound of women being raped. The cries of children. The startled shouts of men. Mortal anguish as swords and knives drove home.

The house of Eirini was singled out. Eleni was dragged out of sight by soldiers. The children were given no mercy and their minder Minas had to watch as her charges were put to death. They then put her out of her misery. Villagers who tried to come to the aid of Eirini were also attacked and killed.

After the retreat of the soldiers a heavy pall of smoke hung over Crete.

A long silence.

It would be many days since this carnage would be forgot. Many days.

THE RAIDING PARTY CONTINUED to Cyprus.

In the early days of their forays out to sea they had relied on a single square sail much like those adopted on Greek merchant ships but later two triangular topsails were placed above it, and a square sail was pushed out over the bow enabling them to use beam winds to their advantage, winds blowing at right angles to their course.

They ate on the move, some of the men eating dormice.

They left Cyprus much as they had left Crete - a shambles.

They continued on. Jerusalem and Antioch and Ephesus beckoned!

They would never get there.

STORMS COULD BLOW UP on the Mare Nostrum with little or no warning.

There was perhaps nothing as frightening as wind-whipped water, no land or refuge or safe harbour within sight, and waves of twenty-five feet and higher. The wood of the boat creaked and groaned like an old man rolling over and over. The sudden movements of the war galley sent things crashing to the decks; glass, wooden objects, quills, personal items. It was like a kaleidoscope of hazards waiting to be discovered.

The soldiers didn't like the conditions, unlike the men of the ship who were more used to working these conditions. Many of the soldiers were ashen-faced and many were seasick.

Caius was in charge of one hundred soldiers, a centurion. At twenty-eight he was young to be a commander but you could see the drive and ambition in his rugged and scarred face. He was a natural leader having being introduced to the concept as a child in Rome.

His men were an assorted lot - good soldiers, bad ones, shirkers, black soldiers, mercenaries from all over. A motley crew.

As the storm picked up four men were suddenly swept away. It happened so fast they didn't even cry out. One minute t here, the next gone. There was no point turning the ship in a futile rescue attempt. The sea had swallowed them whole.

Down in the holds of the boat, the Cypriots captured lay motionless - dead. They no longer had to worry about the storm.

The ship yawned and rolled. The sails ripped. The decks were awash with water.

There was no escaping it.

There was the ragged sound of wood splintering. The wind was howling like a banshee. The rain came in blinding sheets.

It was as if the Roman gods had looked down on all the mayhem left behind the soldiers and declared enough is enough. The Romans worshipped many gods - Mars, Jupiter and Neptune amongst them.

Mars was the Roman God of war and destruction and perhaps he was behind all this mayhem now.

Caius was one of the last to go. It was so unfair, the injustice of it. Gone were his dreams of leading legions into Rome in triumphal displays. He opened his mouth to scream but water drowned out the sound.

He choked.

The seawater hit his lungs. He was gone.

It was a rude awakening for the Roman raiders.

Every manjack of them was dead. Drowned, or washed away.

Had he known of the irony Marc Procus would have smiled. Thankfully for him, he remained oblivious.

He had received word back from Calogero that he could visit upon his return and that a special 'eye' would be kept on Luna and their children. With that he had to be content: what was the alternative? The unthinkable – betray Rome?

CHAPTER 14.

The Vigilis would have been shocked to learn of the events in Crete had he known about them but thankfully he was blissfully unaware and would remain that way for some months to come. Winter would have arrived by the time he learned of Rome's vengeance. And by then everything would have changed including his beliefs in Rome.

Ephesus had opened his eyes to a lot of things. The beauty of the place had staggered him. Although the influence of Rome could be seen in the architecture, especially the Temple of Artemis, the library of Celsus, and even the terraced houses.

Procus knew it to be a place where Saint John had settled following the crucifixion in Jerusalem. He had also seen the little stone house that Mary, the mother of Jesus, had lived in.

He liked this place. It had an energy about it that appealed to his senses and nature. The apostle John preached there and having listened to the man, Procus found his teachings novel. It was John who had stood at the foot of the cross whilst Jesus was been crucified.

To Mary his mother, Jesus had said: "John. Behold your mother!"

Directly to his mother: "Mother, behold your son." It was to John too who was told he would have a long life. It was to John who was told he, alone of the others wouldn't die a martyr's death.

Following the crucifixion John had taken Mary to Ephesus with him and had secured her a stone house in the foothills surrounded by copious trees, a well, and stone pavings. Flowers grew, and fruit.

It was like a place of retreat.

Definitely one of prayer.

It was in Ephesus that he learned how to pray himself.

IT WAS KNOWN AS 'THE Way'.

Some thought of it as a saying from the time of Isaiah: "Prepare the way of the Lord."

In any event it became a saying of Christianity that in order to follow the preaching of Jesus one had to follow the way.

It was a way of life that could be disconcerting. To love one's enemy, to turn the other cheek we're not easy options to adapt or to practice.

For Procus, it wasn't just the Jesus story that fascinated and enthralled but all of the other characters too - John the Baptist, Peter the fisherman and the rock, the doubting tones of Thomas, the betrayer Judas, the apostles, Mary who lived here in Ephesus, Lazarus, and Mary Magdalene. Then there was King David, Abraham, Isaiah, and all the other prophets down through the ages, including the great Moses himself.

He had of course met some of the biblical characters - Pontius Pilate, the Apostle John, and Mary the mother of Jesus, and Peter and his wife. So far of course only the old scrolls existed but he was willing to bet that in time new scrolls and scriptures would exist with Jesus and his ministry taking centre stage. John had told him about some of his writings.

The first biblical story to enthrall him was that of Moses and how he had survived crocodiles and water by placement in a wicker basket on the Nile where he had been discovered by a princess, daughter of the Pharaoh.

Then there was the story of David and how he slew the giant with a catapult and a stone.

And there were the stories of Jesus too - how he had turned water into wine, how he had cured the sick and the crippled, how he had fed the masses with loaves and fish, how he had raised the dead, and how he had walked on water. Incredible!

Or so Marc thought, anyway.

He was aware of a change within him, almost like a conversion. He didn't fight it.

He quite liked this new view of the world; this strange planet they all existed on.

ONE OF THE THINGS THAT the Vigilis had been forced to examine when investigating the murder of Julius Caesar was what role Epicurus had taken in the assassination. Epicurus was a philosopher whose teachings influenced Gaius Cassius Longinus, one of Caesar's assassins and a brother-in-law of Marcus Junius Brutus, better known simply as Brutus, another slayer of Caesar.

He'd noted that Brutus sided with Pompey against Caesar during a civil war in the years 49-45 BC, but subsequent events including defeat in battle brought Caesar more into the limelight and it was considered that the gods were in his favour.

However, Brutus became embroiled in a new plot against Caesar and took a leading role in the assassination. When Caesar's adopted son, Octavian, assumed power, one of his first acts was to name Brutus and Longinus murderers, which led to a second civil was whereby Octavian aligned with Mark Antony fought forces controlled by Brutus and Cassius. The assassins overwhelmed in battle took their own lives.

From what Procus could see the philosophical Epicurus way of thinking stood in direct contrast to the type of power Julius Caesar was trying to amass and could have had a role in the assassination but it was hard to say. Procus didn't know much about Greek philosophy so it was hard to get his head around certain concepts.

He made scrupulous notes of his findings because perhaps somebody more versed in the philosophical concepts might see something he had overlooked. In looking into the death of Caesar he had examined the lives of all the known players. Much of his work had involved going into the great libraries of Rome and examining old papers, scrolls and maps. He also spoke to people, especially experts in the field and historians.

It might have been concluded that there was nothing new to be investigated in the assassination but Rome would still be happy, knowing that they had never given up, and never would.

The soul of Julius Caesar could rest in peace.

CHAPTER 15.

It would be a long time before Procus found out that Michilas and his family had shared the same fate as Eirini and Elini because his ship back across the Mediterranean didn't take in Cyprus. Different strokes, different ships, different agendas. A different course entirely.

Crete didn't look the same.

Eirini and Eleni were gone and there was no sign of the children. Their whitewashed cottage still stood but it was a burnt-out shell.

The faces of the people were different: unsmiling, watchful, suspicious. Cold eyes greeted him everywhere he went but he eventually met one grizzled old man who met his stare. Procus spread his hands. "What happened?"

"They were taken," the old man said.

"Taken?"

"By your people," the man spat out. "By Romans. Ranting and raving like lunatics about Christianity."

Procus felt sudden anger from within. He had left instructions in his reports that these people harboured no threat and were to be left alone. He felt sudden dread. "Who else?" he rasped.

"Who else what?"

"Eirini, Eleni, who else was taken?"

"The children," the old man replied. "And Minas. And a dozen other villagers."

It was all too much.

The eyes of Procus squeezed tight. Tears lurked.

Suddenly Rome didn't matter anymore. Caligula would pay for this treachery, and so too would Juno and Faunus. It was a vow he made to himself.

He felt lucky to escape the place with his life. He knew with certainty that 'taken' meant they had been killed.

RETURNING OVER THE Mediterranean Procus wondered if his Cypriot friends were still alive?

After seeing what happened on Crete, he had a bad feeling about them.

The Romans called the Mediterranean the Mare Nostrum. In truth, they had come to seafaring late and their earlier ships had mirrored the Egyptians and the Carthaginians. When they did come to look seriously at building a fleet, they had the added advantage of using stronger woods in their construction - fir and oak.

They began to experiment with longer and deeper ships, recognising too that a fleet of war galleys could bring in tremendous amounts of plunder. They introduced better sails; triangular, square and topsails. They made their boats so that they could take advantage of different winds, not just a raging one astern.

For perhaps the first time in his life Marc Procus found himself praying. He knew within himself that it was a direct line to God. He prayed that his Cypriot friends hadn't shared the same fate as his Greek ones.

The power of his prayers seemed to reach deep inside, changing him, forging him.

At first, they seemed to give him peace. Acceptance over things he could not change. He was aware of the power of silence too and that of silent prayer, silent meditation. His Christian friends had taught him well. He prayed against the anger that surged through his veins, an anger directed at Rome. He knew now he was right in his decision to return home. However, it would only be home until he gathered Luna and the children and then it would be back east. He had liked the look of Antioch. They would settle there and see where that took them.

CHAPTER 16.

He slipped back into Italy via the port of Messina in Sicily. He needed to be careful here because the emperor had many friends in this part of the world, especially at the harbour where he had created lots of employment. He was wearing his kaffiyeh which concealed everything except his eyes.

He knew Calo lived on the far side of the island and he'd have to hire horses to get there.

He had the Roman eye for a good horse, or horses. The man trying to sell him the horses had pulled a fast one should have been a better judge of character. He offered a sorrel that had seen better days. The violence was shocking and unexpected and it showed the strain that Marc Procus was operating under. It wasn't bad violence; just a slap across the face but it shocked the innocence out of the morning and talk died out. All eyes swung to the horse seller and to the Roman man.

What was going on?

"Are you okay, Tarcus?" one man asked.

"What's happening?" another demanded.

Procus spoke up before things got out of hand. "I'm looking for a good horse."

All eyes swung to the sorry looking sorrel and all understood the reason for the sudden violence. They didn't know he was going to have to kill several good horses to get to his destination by nightfall.

"You should learn to keep your hands to yourself," a man muttered threateningly.

Procus smiled disarmingly. "I should," he agreed, inwardly seething. He didn't need this right now.

HE VIRTUALLY KILLED two horses riding over to Calogero's house. The house looked like a Spanish hacienda and sprawled out sideways and backwards. The trader had given him good horses in the end knowing that to do otherwise would once again bring forth that sudden violence he had been experienced firsthand at the port. Once was enough; and he had furnished two swift-footed palominos.

It was a land of mountains and vineyards and rough, rugged terrain. Wild horses, indigenous to Sicily, roamed in certain spots like the Nebrodi and Madonie mountain range. Perhaps he'd have time to break in a new Sanfratellano horse should the two he'd bought in Messina not be up to the task. He did know he was going to kill them. Parts of the land looked like desert, interspersed with clumps of green and yellow. He would need to negotiate thick forests of Cork trees, beech and oak and yew trees.

Calo was in the yard as he rode in. Other horses milled around.

"Looks like you had a hard ride? Calo observed shrewdly. He flicked his hand towards two servants who immediately moved forward to take hold of the horses. They would be fed and watered and given hay to lie down in.

THE SICILIAN WAITED in the shadows and as soon as he saw his target emerge from the public-baths he slipped in behind him and slipped the garrotte around his neck. The garrotte was a favourite method of execution amongst Sicilians of a certain vintage. It was both effective and personal, and it got the business done.

The steel cut into the man's neck like sliced cheese, making him gasp and choke, his hands trying to reach for the tightening steel around his neck, struggling to breathe, the hands falling limp again. The man's feet kicked, trying to find purchase where there was none. Darkness was closing in fast.

The executioner continued to exert pressure. Experience told him the end was near. The fighting had subsided and the victim seemed to have accepted his fate. The Sicilian knew for sure when the victim's body went limp.

He straightened up, sweat on his forehead as he loosened the garrotte.

The victim hit the ground and lay unmoving.

Even in death, Faunus looked like a rabid rabbi.

The Sicarii turned to two men nearby. "The boat ready?"

"It's ready."

The Sicarii thrust his garrotte into a pocket in his toga and he toed Faunus with his foot. "Take him out deep," he ordered. "It's important he not be found."

The men laughed harshly. "Don't worry," they advised, hoisting heavy chains. "He won't be found. Ever."

They laughed like hungry vultures.

ALTHOUGH BORN INTO the Julio-Claudian Dynasty, the Emperor Caligula was far from secure in his position. He knew certain members of the Senate were against him and wanted to bring back their version of a Roman Republic. He would have been uneasy to learn that certain courtiers and members of the Praetorian Guard were unhappy with his leadership style and were lying in wait to betray him.

He could sense the treachery in the very air.

The Palatine games had been good this year and had given him a false sense of security. He had allowed a relaxation of his guard; men suddenly wanting to get away with their families.

The games were a Roman celebration begun in 249 BC, the second were in 146, and a third set in 17 BC. during the reign of Emperor Augustus.

They were also known as the Secular Games or *'Ludi saeculares'* and consisted of sacrifices and theatrical performances held over three days and nights to mark the end of a saeculum and the beginning of the next. Caligula didn't know he was to be the ultimate sacrifice during this celebration. It was because of the games that the Roman poet Horace composed his famous *'Carmen Saeculare'* or Sacred Hymn.

There would be no special hymns to Caligula. His days were numbered.

In the shadows, men waited to seize the moment and make a play for power.

Powerful men. Dangerous men.

JUNO HAD LEARNED OF the fracas at Messina and close questioning of Tarcus had confirmed suspicions in his mind that Marcus Procus had returned to Italian soil, but why Sicily? What was in Sicily?

The Vigilis had bought two good horses.

Suddenly he knew, he guessed.

Senator Calogero had a house in Sicily and although he had no proof Juno knew the wily Sicilian senator was no friend to the emperor Calogero. Had the Vigilis thrown his hand in with that lot.

Juno's mind raced. Calogero had his associates, both Victoria and Antonia Minor. There were rumours within Rome that he even had the 'ears' of some of Caligula's closest guards.

Juno shivered. Juno was worried. He had reported to Caligula that Faunus had gone missing and he was concerned about it. It wasn't like the man not to keep in touch. Juno suspected foul play and he wished the Vigilis was around so he could investigate. There were other investigators but none could match the extraordinary abilities of Procus. He wondered was there a way Procus could be recalled to Rome.

He'd ask Caligula. He'd put it in a way that there was no sense spending time and money investigating something that might never happen. The Seer hadn't said Rome would be destroyed in their lifetime. Let future emperors worry about it. They had enough to deal with in their own lifetimes. He issued orders to the guard. "Arrest Luna and her children."

The orders came too late.

IN A WAY, IT WAS PROVIDENTIAL that the rescue of Luna and her twin children should fall to the reliable shoulders of Calogero's wife Guilea. Like her husband, Sicilian blood raced through her veins. Her small, oval face made her seem like less of a threat and men found themselves disarmed by her frailty.

She was the type of person that could blend easily and the streets of Rome were no strangers. She moved with ease and poise through the crowds although her dark eyes missed nothing.

She had men with her who were helping her. Sicilians.

One now approached her. "You were right," he hissed. "She's been watched."

"Okay, Paolo," she hissed back. "Keep following and don't let them see you."

Sipping a ca'lida at a tavern Guilea turned the matter over in her mind and decided to take a bold approach. All too well she understood the mindset of the men employed by the emperor Caligula and his sidekick Juno. They were merely brawn, somewhat lacking in the brain department.

All arrangements had already been made. A ship's passage to Sicily. Private carriages. Nothing left to chance.

She decided on the boldest approach. She approached the house of Procus directly. The man guarding the front straightened up.

Guilea knew his type. "My man," she ordered, " fetch Luna Procus immediately and her children."

"What for?" Belligerent tone.

Guilea seemed to lose her patience. "At once, man," she ordered. "At once. Do you know who I am? What's your name?"

"Felix, ma'am," he replied, "and yes I do know who you are. Senator Calogero is your husband."

" He is," she said in a haughty tone, "and he won't be pleased if we're late. Fetch them now please."

Felix didn't know what to do. He was under orders from Juno but Calogero wasn't the type of man to make an enemy of. Guilea looked just as dangerous. He'd answer to Juno later; this was the here and now.

He turned to do Guilea's bidding.

She kept her face straight, no hint of a smile twisting at her lips.

Moments later she was away with Luna and the two children.

They'd find out within the hour of course and pursuit would follow, but Guilea only needed the hour.

By that time, they'd all be safely at sea.

Juno might order a war galley in pursuit but with darkness closing coupled with a sea fog their chances of discovering the party were slim at best.

By morning time, they would be safely ensconced in Calogero's fortress.

Safe from even the emperor's hands.

CHAPTER 17.

The man standing just to the side of the Senators gave Procus a shock. Gneus Spurius - second-in-command of the Praetorian Guard. Only Cassius Chaeria was above him and with a shock he saw Chaeria was there too.

Had Calogero betrayed him?

Antonia Minor caught his expression and guessed at the cause. He smiled and introduced Marc Procus to Gneus Spurius and Cassius Chaeria, the three men shaking hands and eying one another curiously having heard of each other.

Suddenly he knew why they were there. Spurious was smaller than Chaeria, with a wild, bulldog look whilst Chaeria was tall for a Roman with perhaps a hint of Hispania blood. It was obvious both were military men.

"You're planning to assassinate the emperor?"

"I take it you don't approve?" Cassius was blunt.

Procus was equally blunt. "Prior to my current assignment, I've just spent the last six months examining the circumstances surrounding the death of Julius Caesar. My conclusions on such things are that things are best left alone."

"Two different men," Spurius interjected. "Two different emperors. Two different leaders."

"He's just back from Gaul," Calo observed.

Antonia Minor clapped his hands. "And probably not expecting trouble. His guard might be down at the games." Indeed, they might.

The tall, ramrod figure of Victoria was suddenly there with his wife Lucia. "The games?" Victoria asked?

"The games," Antonia Minor announced in his heavy accent. His wife Drusilla had just appeared alongside him. Calogero also approached.

Procus nodded and put a question to the Sicilian. "Guilea?" he smiled back. "She's been sent on a mission of the highest importance. To rescue your Juna and your twin children."

Procus stammered his thanks.

"Nonsense, my man," Calo replied. "We look after our own."

THE PALATINE GAMES.

Caligula knew he had allowed his guard down. The games were a religious festival involving sacrifices and theatrical performances to Roman deities on the Palatine and Capitoline Hills. He had slipped away from his regular guards to approach some actors and at the last minute he noticed that they were not who they seemed to be. Wasn't that Cassius Chaeria, drawing a sword from beneath his toga.

Caligula understood immediately. An assassination. Something he had feared ever since taking up the throne. It didn't seem fair. He was only twenty-eight.

The sword sliced into his body making him gasp and turn rigid with shock. He was aware of other strikes, knives and swords doing the dirty work. There was pain all over. He cried out one final time and then he died. He fell to the floor.

Claudius was waiting nearby.

Cassius approached him. "It's done, emperor."

"Very well," Claudius acknowledged. Orders were quietly given. Arrests made. Someone always had to pay for the death of an emperor. The two guards looked at Claudius aghast. "We thought you were with us?"

Claudius shook his head and didn't answer. He looked to his own guard. "They are to be executed immediately."

That would be an end to it. Calogero and the other senators wouldn't face any justice - they were too powerful. But proletarian guards, turned traitors, they were expendable. Spurious and Chaeria were led away.

Claudius gave further orders. "Clean up here. Accord him the respect of his rank and let us enter a period of mourning."

Claudius knew that meant nine days of mourning. Caligula's household would wear black and daily routines would cease for the nine-day period. In truth, many would have secretly rejoiced at the news as during his reign Caligula had changed from a moderate man to one so openly cruel as to leave his closest allies appalled. Nevertheless, people would exchange their white toga to a black one.

The funeral service would commence with the praeficae, a group of mysterious women who lived near the Libitina, a temple dedicated to the funerary goddess. The women would begin chanting and self-mutilating, their initial cries taken up by members of Caligula's household. The praeficae were hired to begin the mourning, the lamentations and the nenia, a type of funerary song praising the life of the deceased.

Forbidden to take part in any of the mourning ritual it was encumbrant upon a male relative to deliver a eulogy, praising the good deeds of the deceased. Often, the eulogy was a platform for something greater, a launchpad for a political grab. It was also known as the 'lauditio funebris'.

What followed were games, often gladiator fights to the death, followed by a lavish feast some days later.

Calogero, his role unknown in Caligula's demise, moved though the throng gauging the reactions of the ruling classes. The treachery within reigned like his Sicilian blood.

Calogero had his own dreams for Rome but he doubted they would come through. He knew from what people were saying. They'd only accept so much change.

His ways were the old ways. Gone, forever.

THE NEW EMPEROR, CLAUDIUS, began his reign in 41 AD. by rounding up all the inner circle of his predecessor Caligula thereby creating new opportunities and employment for his own people. Most accepted the change as part of the life. There would always be dissenters and Juno was one of the most vociferous.

"This is an outrage," he protested. "I'm not without influence."

"Enough, Juno," a soldier ordered, tying his wrists.

"What will happen to us?" Juno asked.

A grim hint of amusement hit the face of the soldier and his tones were mocking when he replied: "There's games coming up, isn't there?"

"Games?"

"To mark the accession of Claudius?"

Juno's face fell. There was nothing more to be said. They were to feature at the games - the lions.

ROME!

The Roman poet Tibullus crowned it 'The Eternal City' in the 1st century BC. There are legends that surround the birth of Rome as a city including that of two brothers suckled by a she-wolf - Romulus and Remus. Romulus reportedly killed Remus following an argument over the construction and Rome was named after Romulus. Other legends contend that Rome was founded by Aeneas, an escaped Trojan. Some say it was founded by Evander of Pallantium, a Greek cultural hero, who supposedly settled with his people - the Arcadians.

The Roman poet Tibullus crowned it 'The Eternal City' in the 1st century BC. There are legends that surround the birth of Rome as a city including that of two brothers suckled by a she-wolf - Romulus and Remus. Romulus reportedly killed Remus following an argument over the construction and Rome was named after Romulus. Other legends contend that Rome was founded by Aeneas, an escaped Trojan. Some say it was founded by Evander of Pallantium, a Greek cultural hero, who supposedly settled with his people - the Arcadians. From around 753 BC. Rome was controlled by Etruscan Kings for several hundred years, and in 509 BC. an oligarchic republic was established which led to internal struggles between aristocrats known as patricians and plebeians or small landowners. Rome also became embroiled in struggles and wars against populations of Central Italy including Latins,

Etruscans, Volsci, Aequi and the Marsi. In time, Rome consolidated all of its power over all of Italy and beyond, becoming unconquerable in the process.

AND THIS WAS THE MONSTER he had to overcome, to betray. It was little wonder that his fingers trembled at the thought and that his insides turned to jelly. Throughout the years, others had tried to take on Rome - the story of Spartacus and his rebel army springing most readily to mind. Spartacus had led a slave revolt resulting in some serious victories before Rome responded with Crassus and his legions. By 71 BC. it was all over and Spartacus lay dead in battle and his supporters crucified all along the Appian Way.

Rome could be cruel, no two ways about it. For a long time now they had practiced crucifixion. Following the revolts of Spartacus thousands were crucified. In 4 BC. the Roman general Varus crucified two thousand Jews. Crucifixion itself was regarded as a shameful way to die and was applied to criminals, disgraced soldiers, Christians and foreigners, but rarely to Roman citizens. Some said it had its origins in the Assyrians or Babylonian cultures and it was thought that Alexander the Great brought it to east Mediterranean countries and that Phoenicians introduced it to Rome proper. In the 6th century BC. the Persians had also used it, and from them it had spread.

Scourging often preceded crucifixion whereby the victim would receive the lash thirty-nine times, often exposing underlying tissue and bone. It was a very bloody affair. Cicero, who had witnessed many crucifixions was quoted as saying "that most cruel and disgusting penalty". Often, and sometimes to hasten death which could take up to six days the legs of the victim were broken with a club, a process known as crurifragium.

It was often incumbent upon the soldiers to stay until the crucified were indeed dead hence the reason they got bored and tried to expedite matters by lancing and spearing or by lighting fires at the base of the cross to hasten asphyxiation with smoke. Afterwards the body was taken down for burial but sometimes it was left as a deterrent and a warning to those who opposed Roman rule.

Cicero was known as one of Rome's great orators. A philosopher, politician and lawyer he came from a wealthy background of the Roman Equestrian order.

The thing about the emperor is that he had nowhere to go. Once appointed that was it. He couldn't ascend to any higher office. He was suddenly a target for everyone else. Juno understood that and it was the reason why he would never step into those shoes himself. He was happier working in the background.

Rome was known for its great orators, politicians, philosophers, writers and poets. Wasn't it Virgil who had penned the Aenead? In many ways they modelled themselves after their Greek counterparts - the great philosopher Socrates for example. The great language of Rome was Latin. Curiously enough, the Roman historian Suetonius claimed that no less a personage than Julius Caesar had mostly spoken Greek during his lifetime.

Rome had many enemies. At first Caligula had been a benign emperor but something in his personality had changed.

It was why his people were turning upon him, wishing him gone, wishing him dead.

It had happened before with Julius Caesar when Pompey, who had drawn closer to the senatorial establishment and in the process making himself an enemy of Julius Caesar. Brutus too had turned against his emperor.

Born in Suburra in Ancient Rome in 100 BC. Julius Caesar was a soldier and a politician before becoming emperor. He had a string of victories in the Gallic Wars, he built a bridge across the Rhine and he was responsible for invading Britannia . Between 45 and 49 BC. Caesar challenged his Senate's authority by engaging in a civil war that left him virtually unchallenged. Some of his new programs included the introduction of the new Julian calendar, widespread land reform, new citizenship but in early 44 BC. when he was declared 'dictator perpetuo', men grew fearful of his dominance and power and on the Ides of March, the fifteenth of the month, he was assassinated leading the way for Augustus to take command.

Caligula was no Julius Caesar, nor an Augustus, nor a Tiberius. His reign was destined to be a short one. Over time, his extravagance grew and so too did his sexual perversions that included incest with his sisters. He'd never done it with Juno but he was also known to allow the parading of women married to the men of his court and he would pick what he perceived as the best to accompany him to his royal chambers. Say no more!

The Romans having sacked the great cities of Corinth in Greece and Carthage of North Africa were in a pole position to reinforce their own unique way of living with regard to laws, constitutions and elections. Roman engineering was second to none with giant aqueducts being built, and engineering was to the fore when building the great roadways, like the Appian Way which stretched from Rome to Southern Italy or the Via Domitia which stretched into Hispania. Roman architecture was very evident also such as the Pantheon.

The empire would in time stretch as far north as Hadrian's Wall in Brittany's before meeting the Picts of Caledonia – Scotland. The term 'Picts' derived from the Latin word Picti which meant painted warriors, and the term Picti was first coined by the Roman orator Eumenius. The empire also stretched south taking in Northern Africa. Conquered territories included Gaul, Germania, and the eastern empire which included places like Judea and Ephesus. It was said that the empire stretched from the Nile to the Rhine and it wasn't an idle boast.

Slaves drove the economy: picked the olives, quarried the stone, mining the silver mines of Southern Hispania, building the temples. Olive oil also drove the economy.

Roman coinage depicted the head of the emperor. Gods too were depicted on the coinage. Rome's food consisted of fish like mussels and oysters, seasoned meats, seasonal vegetables, legumes, flatbreads, olives and wines. Fresh fruits were also enjoyed and foods like figs. Julius Caesar's favourite dish – borjomi – was pig's neck baked with apples. Salt was used to flavour foods, and spices from the east. Drinks could include Pisca, a mix of vinegar diluted. Beer was considered a barbarian drink and was scorned.

The Romans were energised by everything Greek and tried to emulate them in every way.

Roman maps were long scrolls showing Rome right at the centre and all roads exiting the eternal city. Journeys were often etched on tin mugs, showing mileage to the next service stop and showing total mileage from city to city. On plates and bowls, the Roman way of life was depicted whether that be a rural or urban scene.

The Romans had a penchant for the games, filling vast arenas to watch gladiator fights, or to see people wrestle with wild animals. Chariot races were also big events and attracted large crowds. The development of cities encouraged the construction of amphitheatres, forums, stone temples and fountains. Libraries and centres of culture were encouraged. Plays were supported especially when the right taxes were paid to Caesar. Public baths were encouraged and were used for socialising.

Rome also had the Circus Maximus which held athletic events, chariot racing, gladiator fights, historical re-enactments like that of Troy, horse racing and staged beast hunts.

With such a powerhouse commanding events, was it any wonder that Rome gave pause to Marc Procus? Gave pause too, to enemies like Calogero, Victoria and Antonio Minor.

All three were currently conspiring against the emperor.

Rome was not to be trifled with.

Perhaps Spurius and Chaeria should have known better. It was folly to take on the night of Rome and to betray an emperor.

Rome would never stop looking. Look at that Marc Procus affair. What if the Vigilis unearthed something new?

What could Rome do?

All participants would be dead at this stage. But their descendants would be alive.

As it turned out, Rome could do quite a lot. Lands of participants could be confiscated. Descendants of participants could still pay a heavy price. They could lose Roman citizenship which as well as a loss of rights and privileges could make them eligible for crucifixion.

LUNA RAN TOWARDS MARC as soon as she saw him and they embraced, the children joining them. Calogero's eyes caught those of Guilea. "Any trouble?"

"None, Enna," she confirmed, with a smile. "The fog last night really helped."

"I had people waiting," he advised. "If they had landed, it would have been a bloodbath."

Marc hugged Luna tightly. "It's over," he assured her. "We're safe."

CHAPTER 18.

He liked living in Ephesus.

He had heard about Caligula's death in Rome and that Claudius was the new emperor. New emperors had no interest in the cases that had preoccupied their predecessors and word reached the ears of Marc Procus that he was safe from Rome's power.

Safe, and free to do what he wanted.

Calo had been prevented in the end from establishing a new Roman Republic. It was a step too far. He had suspected that would be the case. The people of Rome did not want to go back to the old days, and the old ways. Time had marched on.

Rome would always have new plots as different dynasties struggled for power. It would remain a powderkeg. He was glad to be free of it.

The old ways, that of being a Vigilis, we're gone and he no longer did that kind of work. He had found work in a local school and he enjoyed passing along his knowledge. He taught history and geography and was sometimes surprised at how Rome occupied so much of his talks and his teachings.

Ephesus was quite a busy sea trading port but it was more laidback than Rome. The majority of its people followed the new movement of Christianity. His boy, Calus was beginning to gain height at seven years of age and his daughter Cala at the same age of course was still her diminutive self.

Calus was beginning to show an interest in ball games - games like harpestum, a game played with a small softball stuffed with feathers, in two halves of the field, the players on each side tackling one auto retrieve the ball and racking up points by bringing it over to their own side of the pitch. The game normally preceded the baths.

Even in a place like Ephesus, far removed from Rome, the influence of Rome was highly evident. One could see it even in the architecture. Giant pillars of marble helped form the temple of Artemis. Roman influence could also be seen in the Library of Celsus and the Great Theatre, and even in the terraced houses. Many of the houses were adorned with flowers and plants and the streets looked colourful; the deep azure of the Mediterranean was never far away.

He remembered the dreams that had once warned
him he might live here. How eerie!

His thoughts were interrupted by Luna. "Marc...there's a man to see you outside."

"Show him in Luna."

The man's frame stooped through the doorway. Half of the interior lay in the open under the deep blue skies although it could be covered with tent-like material in the event of inclement weather.

The stranger was speaking, introducing himself. "You might not know me," he said, "but I'm Iosanas."

The name was familiar to Procus. "You're the seer?" he exclaimed. "The one who warned Caligula that Rome was under threat from the Christians."

"And you're the Vigilis, the one man entrusted to ascertain just how much of a threat they pose?"

"They don't pose any threat."

Iosanas smiled. "You seem very sure of that."

"I am."

Iosanas shook his head as though at the folly of man. "It might not occur in your lifetime or even that of Calus and Cala but eventually Christianity will win over Rome."

Procus went on the defensive. "Leave my children out of it."

"Very well," Iosanas agreed.

"What makes you so sure?"

"I'm a seer, don't forget. My powers have been passed down to me through the ages, from a man known as Nabu."

"You really believe that, don't you?"

"I do."

The seer was busy with papers and scrolls. "I'd like to leave these with you. They're very historic. Perhaps some day you'll cast your eye over them."

"Why me?" Marc asked. "Why trust me with your ancient scrolls?"

"Who better than you, to trust?" Iosanas asked, with a smile. "The man appointed by Rome to investigate the murder of Julius Caesar."

MUCH LATER, WHEN NIGHT had fallen and Luna had put the children to bed and retired herself and he was alone, Marc Procus slowly reached for the old, ancient scrolls and spread them out across the table. The instincts of the Vigilis were kicking in like a good brandy in the stomach. The room was lit by a lamp made from pottery with a linen wick which burned olive oil. It gave sufficient light for the Vigilis to be able to see and take notes.

Quite a few hours went by before he looked up bleary-eyed and yawned.

He had been reading about a man called Nabu and his brilliant student Nebuchadnezzar.

Their words and teachings reached through the years and still resonated.

Perhaps it would be that way with Christianity. Perhaps in the future the Roman Empire would cease to exist. It had happened to other cultures. The Etruscans, the Mesopotamia, the Egyptians, the Minoans, the Celts, the Persia period, and the Hellenistic period and earlier periods of Greek history. Perhaps Christianity would take over. Procus couldn't see it happening in his lifetime but at some point, in the future - who knew?

It was time for bed.

THE END.

Don't miss out!

Visit the website below and you can sign up to receive emails whenever Liam Robert Mullen publishes a new book. There's no charge and no obligation.

https://books2read.com/r/B-A-HWRD-ILHQC

BOOKS 2 READ

Connecting independent readers to independent writers.

Also by Liam Robert Mullen

A Larry Lir
The Secrets of Age

Biblical
The Scribe
Vigilis

Irish
The Nationalists

Larry Lir
Orphans

Sorting out

Sorting out Charlie

Watch for more at
https://www.freelancer555@wordpress.com.

About the Author

An Irish writer from Dublin living in Wexford - Ireland's sunny southeast or so they say. My books and novellas include The Soaring Spirit, Kolbe, The Briefcase Men, Wings, Digger, Land of Our Father, The Scribe, The Nationalists, War, Pacific Deeps, Atlantic Deeps, Mano, Manhunt, Plainclothes, Narc, Sorting out Charlie, Orphans, Paddy, King Brian, Exile, The Department, Precinct, Chief Mano, and other titles. Audio versions of some books are available on ACX. Some of my books have also been translated into Spanish, Portuguese and Italian through Babelcube. My handles include: freelancer555.wordpress.com

www.facebook.com/Liam/Mullen/

Author@irishwriter112

Milton Keynes UK
Ingram Content Group UK Ltd.
UKHW040702201123
432908UK00001B/39